for Viktor

First published in Switzerland under the title Klein-Mannchen hilft einem Freund

First published in the United States, Great Britain, Canada, Australia and New Zealand in 1986 by North-South Books, an imprint of Rada Matija AG.

Distributed in the United States by
Henry Holt and Company, Inc., 521 Fifth Avenue,
New York, New York 10175.
Library of Congress Catalog Card Number: 86-60488.

ISBN 0-8050-0036-4

Distributed in Great Britain by
Blackie and Son Ltd, 7 Leicester Place,
London WC 2H 7BP.
British Library Cataloguing in Publication Data

Velthuijs, Max
Little man to the rescue.
I. Title II. Klein-Mannchen hilft
einem Freund. *English*
833'.914[J] PZ7

ISBN 0-200-72895-4

Distributed in Canada by
Douglas & McIntyre Ltd., Toronto.
Canadian Cataloguing in Publication Data available in
Marc Record from National Library of Canada.
ISBN 0 88894 776 3

Distributed in Australia and New Zealand by
Buttercup Books Pty. Ltd., Melbourne.
ISBN 0 949447 26 9

Printed in Germany

MAX VELTHUIJS

Little Man to the Rescue

Translated by Rosemary Lanning

North-South Books
New York London Toronto Melbourne

Frog was swimming in the river.
The water was clear and cool
and Frog was enjoying himself.

“What a wonderful life,” he sang.
But what was that he saw?

A green bottle was floating past him, bobbing slowly downstream.

With all his might Frog heaved the bottle onto the river bank. There was a piece of paper inside it. Overcome with curiosity, Frog tried to squeeze himself into the bottle.
But he was a bit too fat for this, and got stuck in the bottle's neck.

Just then Little Man happened to walk past.

"Hello, Frog. What are you doing in there?" he said.

"Help! Get me out, please!" groaned Frog. "I can't move backwards or forwards!"

Little Man took hold of Frog's legs and started to pull. This wasn't easy, and it was very painful for Frog. But suddenly he popped out of the bottle like a cork. He was still clutching the paper in both hands.

Little Man took the paper and read it.
"Out loud, please," said Frog impatiently.
Little Man read out, "Help! Help!"
"What else does it say?"
"There's nothing else. Someone needs help. We must go to him at once."
And so the two of them began to walk upstream.

After a while, Frog climbed onto Little Man's shoulders to look around. There was no one to be seen except Duck, who was out for a walk.

"Excuse me, Duck," said Little Man. "Do you need help?"

"No, I'm quite all right, thank you," she replied. Little Man told her about the message in the bottle.

"I'll come and help, too," said Duck. So off they went along the river bank until...

they found Mother Rabbit standing at the water's edge, crying bitterly.

"What's the matter?" asked Little Man. "Do you need help?"

"Father Rabbit went fishing early this morning," she sobbed, "and hasn't come back."

"Then all is explained," said Frog. "It's our friend Rabbit who needs help."

So they all went on together to rescue Rabbit.
Mother Rabbit brought along a basket of provisions

for the journey. They searched and searched,
but Rabbit could not be found.

After a while the path went into a dark forest,
but there was still no sign of Rabbit.
The Rabbit children were frightened.
They had never been so far from home before.

Then they came to some high mountains. Should they go any further? Of course they must! If a friend is in need you can't let him down!

They walked on and on for hours. And when they had almost given up hope of finding Father Rabbit the smallest child suddenly cried: "There he is! There he is!" And there, sitting on a rock on the other side of the river, was Father Rabbit.

“What happened? Have you hurt yourself? Is it serious?” they asked, all speaking at once.

“I fell down, off a cliff,” said Rabbit. “And now I can’t walk.”

If he couldn't walk, he wouldn't be able to swim either. Everyone tried to think of a way to get Rabbit across the water.

"We'll build a bridge," said Frog.

"We'll make a raft," said the children.

"I'll carry him on my back," said Duck. That seemed like a sensible idea.

Duck swam to the far side of the river and Rabbit climbed onto her back. Then she swam back very carefully, like a stately ship. She and Rabbit were greeted with cries of joy on their return, and Little Man looked at the injured leg and put a bandage on it.

A stretcher was quickly made to carry Rabbit, and they walked home in procession, singing

and laughing because they were so happy that
Rabbit was safe.

When at last they were home again, everyone made a great fuss over Rabbit. They all brought him lovely presents, and Mother Rabbit baked him his favourite cake.

The children played him music, and everyone was happy… except Frog.

“What’s the matter?” asked Little Man.

“I’m crying because I haven’t hurt my leg,” said Frog. “If I had, you’d have given me presents, too.”

“But Frog, you still have your beautiful green bottle!”

“I’d forgotten all about that!” said Frog, cheering up at once, and he ran off to look at his newly found treasure once again.